HERE COMES KATE!

First Steck-Vaughn Edition 1992

Copyright © 1989 American Teacher Publications

Published by Steck-Vaughn Company

Library of Congress number: 89-3573

Library of Congress Cataloging in Publication Data.

Carlson, Judy.
  Here comes Kate!

  (Real readers)
  Summary: A girl in a wheelchair learns when to go fast and when to slow down.
  [1. Wheelchairs—Fiction. 2. Physically handicapped—Fiction] I. Kibbee, Gordon, ill. II Title. III. Series.
PZ7.C216626He   1989   [E]   89-3573

ISBN 0-8172-3515-9   hardcover library binding

ISBN 0-8114-6713-9   softcover binding

          4 5 6 7 8 9 0   96 95 94 93

HERE COMES KATE!

by Judy Carlson
illustrated by Gordon Kibbee

RSVP
RAINTREE
STECK-VAUGHN
PUBLISHERS
The Steck-Vaughn Company

Austin, Texas

Kate was fast, fast, fast. In her wheelchair, she could zip down the sidewalk as fast as a race car. Zip! There went Kate!

"Want to race?" she asked her friends. When they raced down the hill, Kate would win.

Yes, Kate was fast.

But sometimes she was too fast. She just could not go slow.

"Kate, try and slow down. Oh no! There goes my birdhouse!" her brother Bruce said.

CRASH!

When Kate called, "Here I come!" all her friends ran to get out of Kate's way. She raced along the streets and down driveways. Sometimes things got in her way. When they did CRASH! Outside, she crashed into trash cans, rose beds, and piles of leaves.

Inside, she was just as bad. She would tip over chairs and crash into beds. She just could not go slow!

"We know that going fast makes you happy," Kate's mom said.

Her dad said, "But we can't be happy when the chairs crack and the beds shake. So, please, slow down!"

"Think slow," said Bruce.

Kate would try to think slow. But sometimes she still went too fast. She just could not go slow!

One day Kate saw a race on TV. This race had wheelchair racers in it. They were fast! They blasted down the streets, their wheels flashing.

Kate rushed outside and raced up and down. CRASH! She ran into the roses and the birdhouse Bruce had just fixed.

"KATE!" her dad yelled. "My roses!"

"KATE!" Bruce yelled. "You broke my birdhouse again!"

"Sorry!" said Kate. And she was! But what could she do? She just could not go slow!

That night when Kate was in bed, her mom came in.

"Kate, there's a time to be fast and a time to be slow," her mom said.

"I know," said Kate.

"You know, if you could find a way to slow down at home, we could go to some races and meet some real wheelchair racers," her mom said.

"Wow!" said Kate. "They may have some tips for me! And maybe someday I could be in a wheelchair race!"

So Kate had to think of a way that she could slow down. And she did.

"What a good plan!" her mom said when Kate told her.

Kate and her mom worked all the next day on Kate's plan. Her dad and Bruce laughed when they saw what Kate and her mom had made. There were signs all over the house. They said, "SLOW!" "2 MPH" "STOP!"

"If I go too fast, Mom will give me a ticket," Kate said.

"But if Kate can go two weeks without getting a ticket, I will take her to some real races," said her mom.

"Then I can find out all about wheelchair racing!" Kate said.

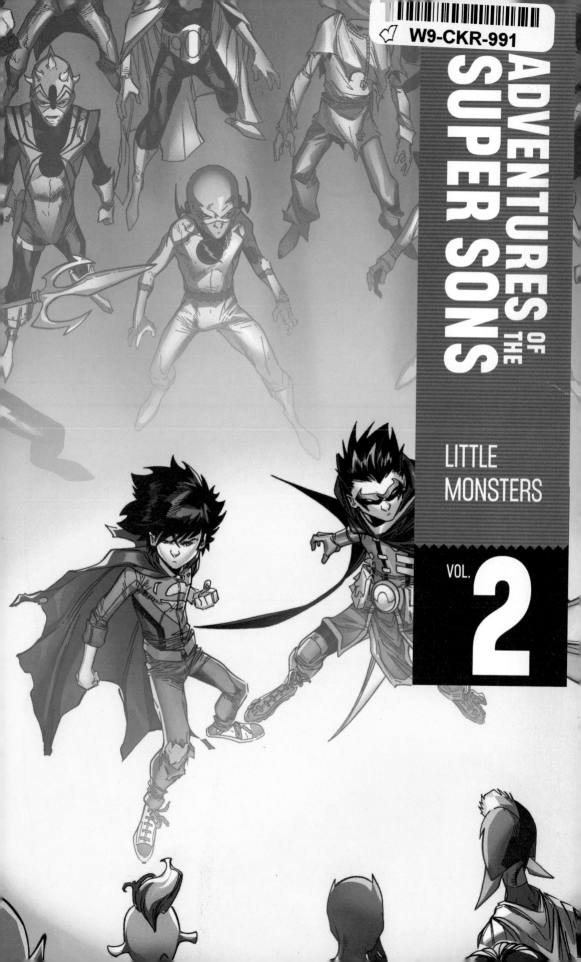

ADVENTURES OF THE SUPER SONS

LITTLE MONSTERS

VOL. **2**

ADVENTURES OF THE SUPER SONS

LITTLE MONSTERS

writer

PETER J. TOMASI

pencillers

CARLO BARBERI
SCOTT GODLEWSKI

inkers

MATT SANTORELLI
SCOTT GODLEWSKI

colorist

PROTOBUNKER

letterer

ROB LEIGH

collection cover artist

DAN MORA

SUPERMAN created by **JERRY SIEGEL** and **JOE SHUSTER**
SUPERBOY created by **JERRY SIEGEL**
By special arrangement with the Jerry Siegel family

VOL.

2

PAUL KAMINSKI Editor – Original Series
ANDREW MARINO Associate Editor – Original Series
DAVE WIELGOSZ Assistant Editor – Original Series
JEB WOODARD Group Editor – Collected Editions
ERIKA ROTHBERG Editor – Collected Edition
STEVE COOK Design Director – Books
MONIQUE NARBONETA Publication Design
CHRISTY SAWYER Publication Production

BOB HARRAS Senior VP – Editor-in-Chief, DC Comics
PAT McCALLUM Executive Editor, DC Comics

DAN DiDIO Publisher
JIM LEE Publisher & Chief Creative Officer
BOBBIE CHASE VP – New Publishing Initiatives & Talent Development
DON FALLETTI VP – Manufacturing Operations & Workflow Management
LAWRENCE GANEM VP – Talent Services
ALISON GILL Senior VP – Manufacturing & Operations
HANK KANALZ Senior VP – Publishing Strategy & Support Services
DAN MIRON VP – Publishing Operations
NICK J. NAPOLITANO VP – Manufacturing Administration & Design
NANCY SPEARS VP – Sales
MICHELE R. WELLS VP & Executive Editor, Young Reader

ADVENTURES OF THE SUPER SONS VOL. 2: LITTLE MONSTERS

DC Comics, 2900 West Alameda Ave., Burbank, CA 91505.
Printed by LSC Communications, Owensville, MO, USA. 10/18/19. First Printing.
ISBN: 978-1-4012-9507-3

Library of Congress Cataloging-in-Publication Data is available.

ADVENTURES OF THE SUPER SONS
#7

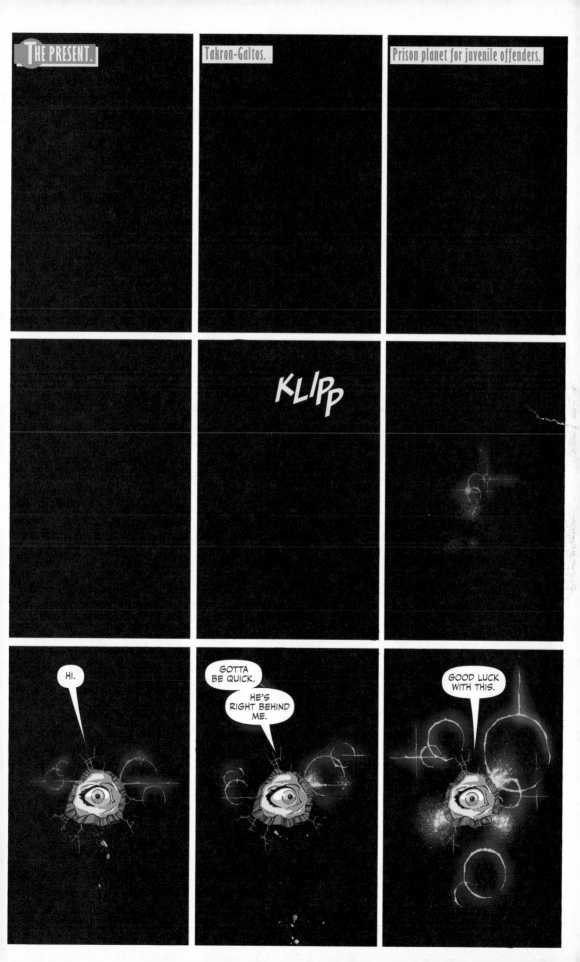

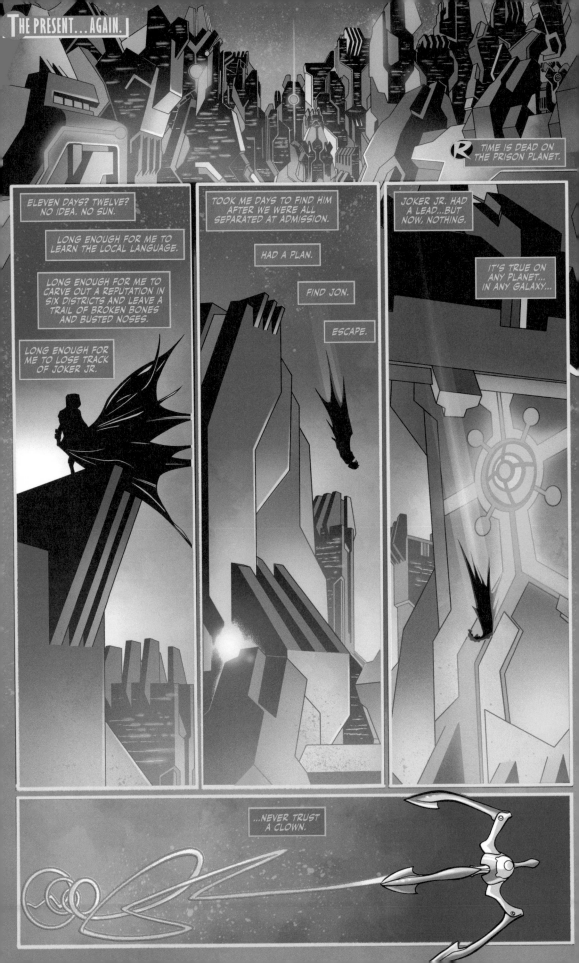

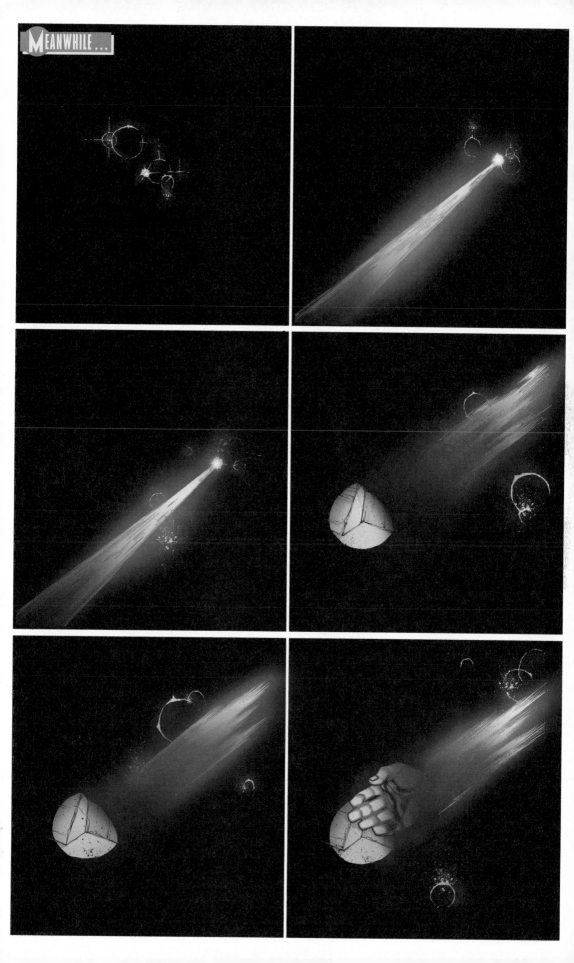

SPILL IT.

WHO'S SEEN HIM?

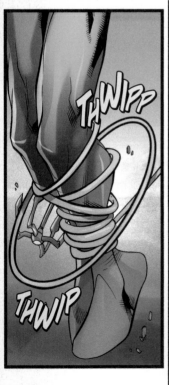

THWIPP

THWIP

YOU BEEN TALKING TO A BALD KID?

TALK!

...Unn... I'M SUPPOSED TO SAY: "WH-WHAT HAS THREE LEGS IN THE...uhh... MORNING..."

R TRIED EVERY STOREFRONT FOR FIVE SECTORS.

NOTHING.

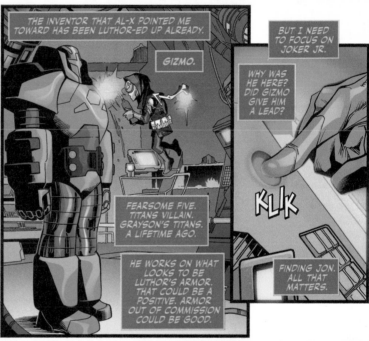

THE INVENTOR THAT AL-X POINTED ME TOWARD HAS BEEN LUTHOR-ED UP ALREADY.

GIZMO.

FEARSOME FIVE. TITANS VILLAIN. GRAYSON'S TITANS. A LIFETIME AGO.

HE WORKS ON WHAT LOOKS TO BE LUTHOR'S ARMOR. THAT COULD BE A POSITIVE. ARMOR OUT OF COMMISSION COULD BE GOOD.

BUT I NEED TO FOCUS ON JOKER JR.

WHY WAS HE HERE? DID GIZMO GIVE HIM A LEAD?

KLIK

FINDING JON. ALL THAT MATTERS.

MY ENTRANCE NEEDS TO BE DRAMATIC.

STRONG.

HAVE TO BE BRUCE-LIKE IN MY INTENS--GAHHH!

...I DON'T KNOW WHERE HE WENT...SWEAR...

...BUT THIS...THIS HERE...IT CAN TRACE ANY OF MY DEVICES. I USE IT FOR SECURITY.

...I CAN SET IT TO TRACK THE SOLAR PLUG I GAVE HIM...

...THAT SHOULD AT LEAST GET YOU *CLOSER*...

MAKE ME TRUST YOU.

THAT LUTHOR GUY... PLANTED SOMETHING INSIDE MY BRAIN.

IT'S HELPED ME CREATE ALL THIS STUFF THE PAST COUPLE CYCLES.

BUT IT HURTS.

IT HURTS SO BAD.

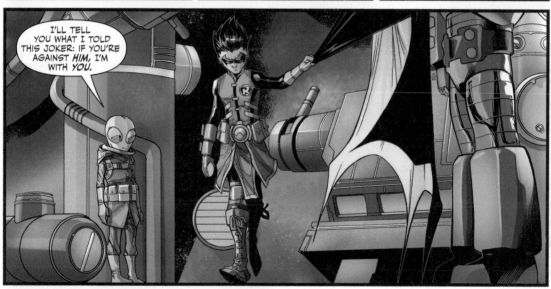

I'LL TELL YOU WHAT I TOLD THIS JOKER: IF YOU'RE AGAINST *HIM*, I'M WITH *YOU*.

YOU SURE AS HELL BETTER BE.

WHAT IS IT, GIZMO?

HE'S GONE.

AND THE ARMOR'S FIXED.

PING PING

MY TRACKER'S TELLING ME I'M CLOSE.

MY MUSCLES TIGHTEN.

I'VE BEEN LED RIGHT TO THE DEVICE. JUST LIKE GIZMO SAID.

BUT WHAT DID JOKER JR. NEED THIS FOR?

WHAT'S HE PLAYING AT?

A SOLAR PLUG, HE CALLED IT.

COULD JON BE--

HEY, RUNT!

KRAP-KOOM

THE WALL EXPLODES OUTWARD.

IT'S POWERFUL.

LIKE A LOCOMOTIVE.

MASK LENS CAKED WITH DUST...BUT MY EARS ARE WIDE OPEN.

AND WHAT I HEAR ISN'T THE CRACK AND CRUNCH OF BROKEN CONCRETE.

NO, I HEAR SIZZLING.

SOMETHING'S HOT AND STILL BURNING.

HI, BUDDY.

ADVENTURES OF THE SUPER SONS
#8

WARNING

WARDEN SNEETCH, THERE'S BEEN SOME KIND OF ENERGY BURST IN SECTOR TWO.

IT'S SOLAR-BASED-- SMACK IN THE MIDDLE OF THE MAXIMUM SECURITY WING.

COULD IT BE--

--THE KRYPTONIAN? WE HAD HIM IN SOLITARY.

GUESS HIS FRIENDS FOUND HIM FASTER THAN WE THOUGHT.

HELLUVA WAY TO COME BACK FROM VACATION.

LET'S SADDLE UP, TROOPS.

TIME TO GO BREAK SOME DELINQUENTS DOWN TO SIZE!

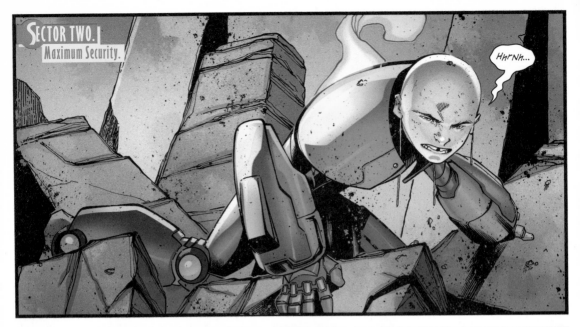

HHRNH...

...JOKER JR.... THIS IS *HIS* FAULT...

...THAT SOLAR DEVICE!

GRRRNN.

YEAH, WELL, YOUR LITTLE BUDDY HIGHTAILED IT OUT OF HERE, SO I GUESS HE AIN'T STICKIN' AROUND TO ACCEPT THE BLAME.

GRARGHH!

SKRUN CH

ROCKED

PETER J. TOMASI · story & words
CARLO BARBERI · pencils
MATT SANTORELLI · inks
PROTOBUNKER · colors
ROB LEIGH · letterer
DAN MORA · cover
ANDREW MARINO · assoc. editor
PAUL KAMINSKI · editor
MARIE JAVINS · group editor

HALF THE PLAN.

HE'S THE OTHER HALF.

HIYA!

I'M *AL-X!* I'M A GREEN LANTERN. WE HAVEN'T MET.

YOU'RE A... *GREEN LANTERN?*

WELL, SORTA... I'M PART OF THE GL CADET PROGRAM.

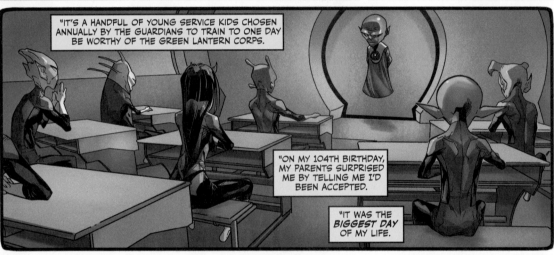

"IT'S A HANDFUL OF YOUNG SERVICE KIDS CHOSEN ANNUALLY BY THE GUARDIANS TO TRAIN TO ONE DAY BE WORTHY OF THE GREEN LANTERN CORPS.

"ON MY 104TH BIRTHDAY, MY PARENTS SURPRISED ME BY TELLING ME I'D BEEN ACCEPTED.

"IT WAS THE *BIGGEST DAY* OF MY LIFE.

"AS PART OF THE TRAINING PROGRAM THEY PLACE US IN JUVENILE DETENTION FACILITIES ACROSS THE UNIVERSE WITH MINIMAL PROTECTION.

"WE CAN EITHER FIND A WAY TO ESCAPE OR SURVIVE. EACH IS ACCEPTABLE.

"IT'S A TEST OF OUR WITS OR OUR STAMINA.

"EITHER WAY, YOU COME OUT LEARNING ABOUT YOURSELF AND WHAT IT TAKES TO BE A MEMBER OF THE CORPS.

ROBIN SAID YOU WERE FROM EARTH... DO YOU KNOW HAL JORDAN?

DID HE SAY 104 YEARS OLD?

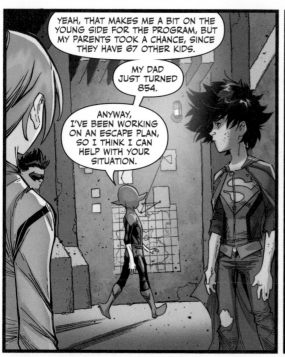

YEAH, THAT MAKES ME A BIT ON THE YOUNG SIDE FOR THE PROGRAM, BUT MY PARENTS TOOK A CHANCE, SINCE THEY HAVE 67 OTHER KIDS.

MY DAD JUST TURNED 854.

ANYWAY, I'VE BEEN WORKING ON AN ESCAPE PLAN, SO I THINK I CAN HELP WITH YOUR SITUATION.

THIS DEAD AREA HOUSES AN INTERPLANETARY DELIVERY SYSTEM THAT CONNECTS TO ONE OF THE OTHER PLANETOIDS IN THIS PARTICULAR HELIX.

TAKRON-GALTOS IS ONLY ONE OF SEVERAL CONNECTED PLANETOIDS, ALLOWING CITIZENS FROM EACH TO TRAVEL QUICKLY AND EASILY BETWEEN THEM.

SAY WHAT NOW?

THEY CALL IT THE VROOM TUBE.

MY RESEARCH SHOWS THAT THIS TUBE IS THE GATEWAY OUT OF PRISON AND ONTO THE NEARBY VACATION PLANETOID.

WHAT IS HE--

HE'S TALKING ABOUT ESCAPE.

YEAH, BUT REX AND DOZENS OF HIS CRONIES ARE OUT THERE LOOKING FOR US.

CORRECTION...

...THEY ALREADY FOUND US.

IT'S ME. PICK UP THE SECURE CONNECTION.

REX? IS THAT YOU? WE BELIEVED YOU TO BE DEAD... OR WORSE.

NO NEED TO WORRY ABOUT ME, BRAINIAC 6. I WAS SIDETRACKED BY THE SUPER SONS AND THE CLOWN, BUT OUT OF THAT CAME JUST WHAT I NEEDED.

YOU, KID DEADSHOT AND THE OTHERS NEED TO COMMANDEER SEVERAL SHIPS AND GET THEM TO THE TAKRON-GALTOS PRISON PLANET.

SEVERAL?

YES. I HAVE FOUND HERE WHAT WE WERE MISSING ON CYGNUS...

...STRENGTH IN NUMBERS.

Hmm?

AND IF YOU HURRY...

...I MIGHT HAVE SOMETHING EVEN MORE SPECIAL.

REX, IT'S ME! I WAS BRINGING THE SONS TO YOU!

JOKER JR.!

HAHAHA!

WHAT YOU THOUGHT WAS A DOUBLE CROSS WAS REALLY A *TRIPLE* CROSS!

A *QUADRUPLE* CROSS!

JUST LIKE WE ALWAYS IMAGINED!

I KNOW EVERYTHING ABOUT THESE GUYS NOW. MADE 'EM TRUST ME BY SAVIN' 'EM!

SURE, YOU GOT A LITTLE HOT UNDER THE ARMOR. BUT IT WAS ALL PART OF A PLAN.

AND WHAT PLAN WAS THAT?

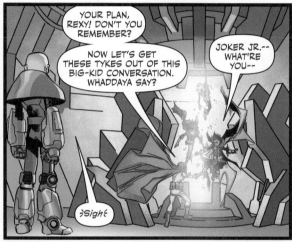

YOUR PLAN, REXY! DON'T YOU REMEMBER?

NOW LET'S GET THESE TYKES OUT OF THIS BIG-KID CONVERSATION. WHADDAYA SAY?

JOKER JR.-- WHAT'RE YOU--

⸮Sigh⸮

AGHH!

FZZAAM

MAYBE THIS TIME YOU'LL *STAY* DEAD.

YOU WANT US TO FOLLOW THE REST OF THEM, MR. LUTHOR?

ADVENTURES OF THE SUPER SONS
#9

SEVERAL DAYS (and four untold adventures) LATER...
THAT PRINCESS BANDIT SURE SEEMED TO LIKE KISSING DAMIAN!
DON'T EVER MENTION THAT AGAIN.
Super Sons in
THE GOOD, THE BAD AND THE SONS

THAT'S JUST YOUR PROGRAMMING TALKING, HEX. BELIEVE ME, I KNOW.

I WAS RAISED AND PROGRAMMED TO DO ONE THING: *KILL.* I HAD NO IDEA WHAT CHOICE WAS AND HAD NO INTEREST IN IT UNTIL...

...WELL... UNTIL FAMILY AND FRIENDS SHOWED ME THERE WAS ANOTHER WAY...THAT I HAD FREE WILL.

THAT'S *YOU,* KID.

IT *AIN'T* ME.

ANYWAYS, I'M GETTING YOU THREE ON THAT TRAIN AND THEN WE CAN ALL GO BACK TO LIVIN' LIKE WE WERE LIVIN'.

THAT'S EASY FOR YOU, HEX. FOR US THAT MEANS SOMEHOW TRYING TO STOP AN ATTACK ON OUR PLANET.

WE GOT AN ENTIRE ARMY OF SUPER-VILLAINS HEADED FOR EARTH.

KID SUPER-VILLAINS.

WHAT'S A *SUPER-VILLAIN?*

LIKE A BAD GUY, BUT WITH EXTRA POWERS.

THIS ALIEN CREEP IS USING A THING CALLED A HYPERCUBE TO CREATE A TON OF NEW ONES INSPIRED BY THE SUPER-VILLAINS ON OUR PLANET.

HE WANTED TO USE KILLING DAMIAN AND ME TO DISTRACT OUR FRIENDS ON EARTH.

WE ESCAPED A BUNCH OF TIMES... BUT HE AT LEAST GOT US OUT OF THE WAY, SO WE CAN'T WARN ANYONE WHAT'S COMING.

SOMEWHERE UP THERE SOME BAD STUFF IS GOING ON. AND WE GOTTA FIND A WAY TO HELP.

ELSEWHERE.

EARTH.

WHAT A *DUMB* NAME FOR A PLANET.

I THINK I'LL RENAME IT.

IF THERE'S ANYTHING LEFT.

EVERYONE IS ASSEMBLED, REX.

EXCELLENT, BRAINIAC. AND GOOD WORK TO THE ENTIRE GANG FOR KEEPING THINGS MOVING WHILE I WAS...DISTRACTED.

I SEE NOW THAT MY OBSESSION WITH JOKER JR. AND THOSE SUPER SONS MAY HAVE BEEN FUN, BUT IT WAS BLINDING ME FROM OUR REAL GOAL.

BUT I'M BACK, FOCUSED AND READY TO LEAD MY...

GRAVEDIGGER TERMINAL.
Engine City.

"LISTEN UP.

"GUARDS ARE MECHS. LIKE ME.

"SO GO ON AND PUT A HURT ON WHOEVER YA WANT."

I STILL THINK WE SHOULD GO EASY ON 'EM. THEY'RE JUST DOIN' THEIR JOB.

YOU ARE SO SOFT. HOW DO YOU EVEN FIGHT CRIME?

AND STOP DROPPING YOUR G'S! YOU LIVE IN METROPOLIS.

SORRY, PARD. RECKON I JES' PICK UP ACCENTS.

ENOUGH JIBBER JABBER, WE GOTTA GET MOVIN' IN THERE.

SHOULDN'T BE TOO HARD, SINCE NO ONE EVER BREAKS IN THROUGH THE EASTERN GATE. IT'S LESS PROTECTED.

YOU GUYS CLEAR OUT THE WAY AND LANTERN HERE'LL FOLLOW.

BUT, HEX, WHAT ABOUT YOU? YOU'RE COMING WITH US, RIGHT?

Nah, GREENJEANS. MY LIFE IS HERE. PROGRAMMING SAYS SO. UNTIL DUTY CALLS AGAIN.

SO YOU'RE JUST WAITING HERE UNTIL THE ARMY COMMANDS YOU BACK TO A LIFE YOU DON'T WANT TO LIVE?

THAT'S NOT DUTY. THAT'S CONTROL.

FIRST OF ALL, KID, YER TRYIN' TO GET INTA THE GREEN LANTERN CORPS, SO YOU CAN SPARE ME THE SPEECHIFYIN' ABOUT PERSONAL FREEDOM.

SECOND... YOU DON'T KNOW NOTHING ABOUT ME.

SOMETIMES IT'S BETTER NOT TO HAVE A CHOICE...

OKAY...

...LET'S GET TO 'EM, KID.

DON'T THINK SO.

WHAT ARE--

KRAK

SKZZT--

KNEW I--

SKZZT--

COULDN'T TRUST--

SKZZT--

A GR--

SKZZT--

--A GREEN LANTERN.

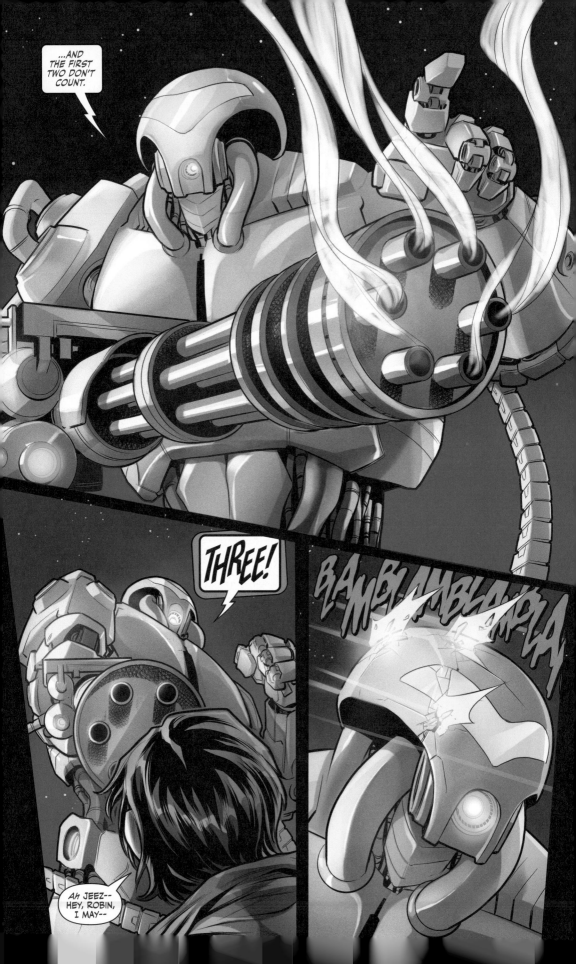

ADVENTURES OF THE SUPER SONS
#10

"THIS IS THE ALMOST-FORGOTTEN STORY THAT SHOOK THE UNIVERSE.

"SUPERBOY AND ROBIN.

"THE 'SUPER SONS,' AS THEY ARE KNOWN IN LEGEND.

"FACING OFF AGAINST THE COMBINED FORCES OF AN ARMY OF NEOPHYTE ALIEN VILLAINS CALLED THE GANG."

"THE YOUNG, OTHERWORLDLY MEMBERS OF THE GANG WERE INSPIRED BY AND NAMED FOR THE VILLAINS OF EARTH.

"DRAWN TOGETHER AND POWERED BY THE ORIGINAL DEVILISH DOPPELGANGER, *REX LUTHOR*...

"...THE GANG HAD GROWN ITS NUMBERS UNTIL THEY NOT ONLY THREATENED EARTH... BUT ALL OF REALITY.

"AND IF THE COMBINED MIGHT OF THE SUPER SONS PROVES TO BE UNEQUAL TO THE THREAT...

"...THEN REX LUTHOR WILL HAVE FINALLY ACCOMPLISHED WHAT HIS COUNTERPART AND SO MANY OTHERS COULD NOT.

"THE DEATH OF A DREAM...

"...THE FALL OF A CIVILIZATION...

"...AND THE RISE OF THE PUREST EVIL.

"THE HOOFBEATS OF HISTORY CRACK THE GROUND OF OUR COLLECTIVE UNCONSCIOUS.

"EACH POUNDING STRIDE TELLS THE STORY OF THE FINAL ADVENTURE OF THE SUPER SONS.

"THE ULTIMATE, CLIMACTIC TALE STARTS HERE...

THE INJUSTICE WAR

WAIT A DANG SECOND!

PART ONE

I'M NOT OVERDOING ANYTHING. *THIS* IS WHAT HAPPENED.

YOUR PARENTS JUST HAVEN'T TAUGHT YOU HOW TO OPEN YOUR MINDS TO THE UNEXPECTED.

THERE WAS A TIME WHEN STUFF LIKE THIS HAPPENED ALMOST EVERY MONTH.

TT

YOU REALLY WANT TO SURPRISE THESE RUNTS?

OH GREAT.

TELL 'EM THE TRUTH.

NOW, WHO ORDERED CHOCOLATE MILK?

ME!!

FINE! YOU THINK YOU'RE BETTER AT EVERYTHING. YOU WANNA TAKE OVER?

FIRST OFF, THERE'S A DIFFERENCE BETWEEN *THINKING IT...* AND *KNOWING IT*, OLD MAN.

SECOND... I *WILL* TAKE OVER. BUT YOU CAN HANG ON TO THE BOOK.

I DON'T NEED TO READ IT.

BECAUSE I LIVED IT.

TRUTH IS, EVERYTHING YOU JUST HEARD THE OLD MAN SAY ABOUT THE SUPER SONS WAS *TRUE.*

AND THE LAST ADVENTURE, IT WAS THE MOST DANGEROUS ONE OF ALL. BUT IT STARTED QUIET.

IT STARTED SIMPLY WITH A PAIR OF THE EVILEST EYES YOU EVER SAW...

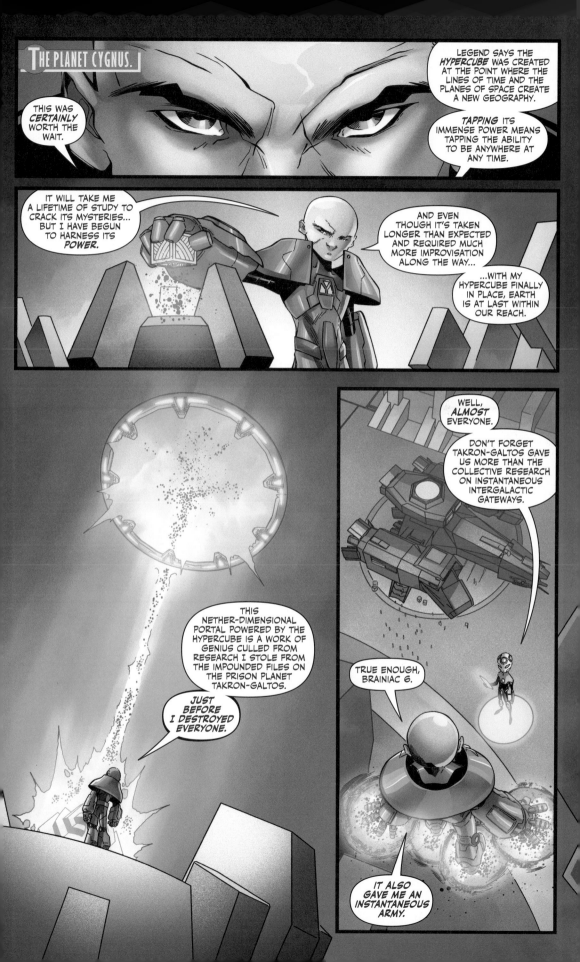

I'M ASSUMING FROM THEIR YELLING WE GOT THE RIGHT PLACE.

YUP. SCANNER SAYS WE'VE ARRIVED AT CYGNUS. WHICH IS NORMALLY A PEACEFUL PLANET ACCORDING TO THE GUARDIANS.

Fhh. **NEVER** TRUST THE AUTHORITIES.

PETER J. TOMASI story & words
CARLO BARBERI pencils
MATT SANTORELLI inks
PROTOBUNKER colors
ROB LEIGH letterer
DAN MORA cover
ANDREW MARINO associate editor
PAUL KAMINSKI editor
JAMIE S. RICH group editor

KID, WE ENTERED THE ATMOSPHERE RUNNIN' HOT. AT THIS SPEED, GRAVITY IS PLAYING HELL ON THE BRAKES.

GET TO THE NEXT CAR AND PREPARE TO UNCOUPLE THE REAR CARS IF WE NEED TO.

BUT I DON'T--

DIDN'T THAT BLASTED GL CORPS TRAININ' TEACH YOU HOW TO THINK ON YOUR FEET?

GO! NOW!

I'M GOING! I'M GOING!

NICE KID, BUT ABOUT AS SHARP AS A SACK OF FEATHERS.

BZZT BZZT

IT'S HEX, TALK TO ME.

YEAH, THAT WAS ME THAT HIJACKED THE TRAIN. LONG STORY. BOTTOM LINE IS I GOT SOMEONE YER GONNA BE MIGHTY INTERESTED IN.

I'M UPLOADING MY MEMORY FILES NOW. COORDINATES WILL FOLLOW.

HEX OVER AND OUT.

MEANTIME, I'LL JUST DO WHAT COMES NATURALLY...

...HUNTIN' BOUNTIES.

WE'RE GOIN' DOWN, YOU IDIOT!

YOU TORE OUT THE BRAKING MECH-- CRASH THIS BIG'LL KILL US ALL!

BLAM BLAM BLAM

I THINK HE'S RIGHT.

WAIT-- DOES THAT MEAN YOU THINK HE'S WRONG?

IT MEANS WE DON'T WANNA BE HERE IN ABOUT TEN SECONDS.

DAMN IT.

WELL, AT LEAST THE KID IS TAKEN CARE OF.

I DID SOMETHING RIGHT.

HEY!

Huh?

OH, IT'S YOU. 'BOUT TIME YOU SHOWED UP.

ADVENTURES OF THE SUPER SONS
#11

PETER J. TOMASI story & words • **CARLO BARBERI** pencils

MATT SANTORELLI inks • **PROTOBUNKER** colors • **ROB LEIGH** letterer

DAN MORA cover • **ANDREW MARINO** & **DAVE WIELGOSZ** corporals

PAUL KAMINSKI captain • **JAMIE S. RICH** general

THEY SAY THE BEST SUMMERS FEEL ENDLESS.

NO!

I WILL HAVE MY INVASION ONE WAY OR THE OTHER!

WHOOSH

I'M ON HIM!

WAIT-- HE MIGHT DRAG YOU TO OUTER SPACE!

POOM

NEEDS OF THE MANY AND ALL THAT STUFF.

I AM STILL THE GREATEST VILLAIN OF ALL TIME!

BETTER THAN ANY OF THEM!

KLIK KLIK

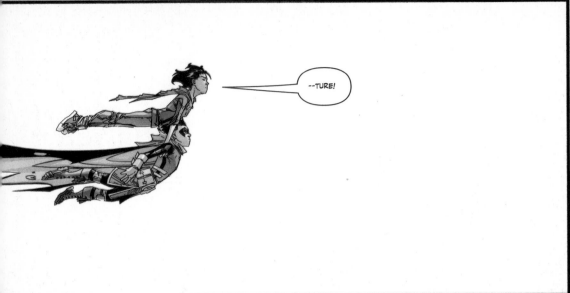

IT HAS SOMETHING TO DO WITH WHAT *"REX"* MEANS ON THEIR PLANET--

HE'S ACTIVATING THE FULL POWER OF THE HYPERCUBE-- *TAKE COVER!*

KING!

ADVENTURES OF THE SUPER SONS

#12

I DID IT.

IT TOOK MY OWN ZETTABYTES OF TECHNOLOGICAL GENIUS MATCHED WITH HUNDREDS OF SACRIFICIAL LAMBS TO DEFEAT THESE JUNIOR SUPER-FOOLS VEXING ME FROM ONE GALAXY TO THE NEXT.

AND NOW I HAVE THESE SUPER SONS *TRAPPED* IN WHAT WAS ALL ALONG MEANT TO BE JUST A TOOL.

BUT I REALIZE THEIR PRISON, THIS *HYPERCUBE*, IS MUCH, MUCH MORE.

THIS IS NO TOOL.

THIS IS A WEAPON.

TIME TO *AIM* IT.

Super Sons in **GANG WAR**
CONCLUSION

PETER J. TOMASI story & words • CARLO BARBERI pencils
MATT SANTORELLI inks • PROTOBUNKER colors • ROB LEIGH letterer
DAN MORA cover • DAVE WIELGOSZ assistant editor
PAUL KAMINSKI editor • JAMIE S. RICH group editor

NNNN...

WHT ESSSSS HPPNIN...?

NGGK!

SUPERBOY SMELLZZZ LLLIKE STINKY BUTT CHEESE.

WILL YOU GROW UP?

HAD TO TEST THE EQUIPMENT.

JUST GET US OUT OF HERE, WOULD YA?

POOPERBOY DROOLS. ROBIN RULES.

I'M A DUMB BALLLD GUY. DUHHHH...

NO!

STOP!

CAN'T LET--

I JUST WANTED TO BE PART OF A STORY... ANY STORY...AND YOURS SEEMED LIKE THE MOST FUN.

YOU GOT SOME STORY, ALL RIGHT. WE JUST NEED TO CLEAN UP THE MESS.

KLIKK

THANK YOU FOR THE INSPIRATION. I'LL ALWAYS REMEMBER MY ADVENTURE WITH THE SUPER S--

THE CUBE! I NEED IT!

WE KNOW *EXACTLY* WHAT YOU NEED, YOU DUMB EVIL DOPPELGÄNGER!

WHAT DAY IS IT?

WHO CARES, IT'S SUMMER...LET'S JUST GET SOME *ZZZZZ...*

YOU MEAN SUMMER OF *SNORRRR...*

OH MAN, THE ARCTIC IS FARTHER AWAY THAN I REMEMBERED.

...SO TIRED...

THERE YOU ARE!

SNOORRZZ-- --hunn--

GAHH!

--ALFRED-- WHAT ARE--

YOUR PARENTS HAVE BEEN WORRIED, BUT I'VE ASSURED THEM YOUR VITAL SENSORS SHOWED THAT YOU WERE IN FINE SHAPE THESE PAST FEW WEEKS.

I KNEW NO MATTER WHAT NONSENSICAL FUN AND GAMES YOU WERE UP TO THIS SUMMER, YOU'D BE BACK IN TIME FOR THE FIRST DAY OF SCHOOL.

FIRST DAY OF SCHOOL?!

YOUR EXCITEMENT FOR THE START OF A NEW SCHOOL YEAR IS QUITE PALPABLE.

WE MISSED THE SUMMER OF SUPER...

Ah, SHADDUP.

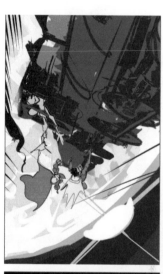

DC UNIVERSE REBIRTH

SUPERMAN

VOL. 1: SON OF SUPERMAN

PETER J. TOMASI with PATRICK GLEASON, DOUG MAHNKE & JORGE JIMENEZ

VOL.1 SON OF SUPERMAN
PETER J.TOMASI * PATRICK GLEASON * DOUG MAHNKE * JORGE JIMENEZ * MICK GRAY

VOL.1 REIGN OF THE SUPERMEN
STEVE ORLANDO * BRIAN CHING * MIKE ATIYEH

SUPERGIRL VOL. 1: REIGN OF THE SUPERMEN

VOL.1 PATH OF DOOM
DAN JURGENS * PATRICK ZIRCHER * TYLER KIRKHAM * STEPHEN SEGOVIA * TOM GRUMMETT

ACTION COMICS VOL. 1: PATH OF DOOM

VOL.1 I AM GOTHAM
TOM KING * DAVID FINCH

BATMAN VOL. 1: I AM GOTHAM